The pattern as adapted for the treble clef, a popular form for vocals.

In memory of
my father, who wanted
to be a singer,
and my grandfather, who
told me the story.

This book is dedicated to
my mother, Willie Louise McNear, who
said to me, "Keep your shoulders back,
hold your head up high, open your
mouth and let the words jump out,"

and to my children,
Aisha, Uhuru, and Jamaal, hoping
they'll keep the frog close to their hearts.

—L.G.

Big love vibe for Emily, Laura, Marcie, Tina, Nicole, Takysha, Deborrah, Paula, Lita, Anna, and Betty! Sing out, sisters!

J.J.

Well, friends, I got a question for you. Have you ever been frustrated? That's right, I said frustrated. Tell the truth now. How do you tell when you are frustrated? Do you feel angry? Do you feel sad? Sometimes you can't sleep. And sometimes you don't want to wake up.
You are *FRUSTRATED*.
Well, then, here's a story for you.

The Frog Who

as told by

Linda Goss

Orchard Books ⊙ New York

Wanted to be A SINGER

illustrated by

Cynthia Jabar

There is this little frog who's feeling mighty bad, mighty sad, mighty mad, and mighty frustrated! Now there's nothing wrong in being a frog. But this particular frog feels that he has talent. You see, he wants to be a singer. And in this particular forest where this particular frog lives, frogs don't sing. Only the birds are allowed to sing.

For a while the frog is cool. He stays to himself and practices on his lily pad, jumping up and down, singing to himself. But one day all of this frustration begins to swell inside him and he says to himself, "I'm tired of feeling this way. I'm tired of holding all this inside me. I've got talent. I want to sing. I can sing, and I'm going to be a singer!"

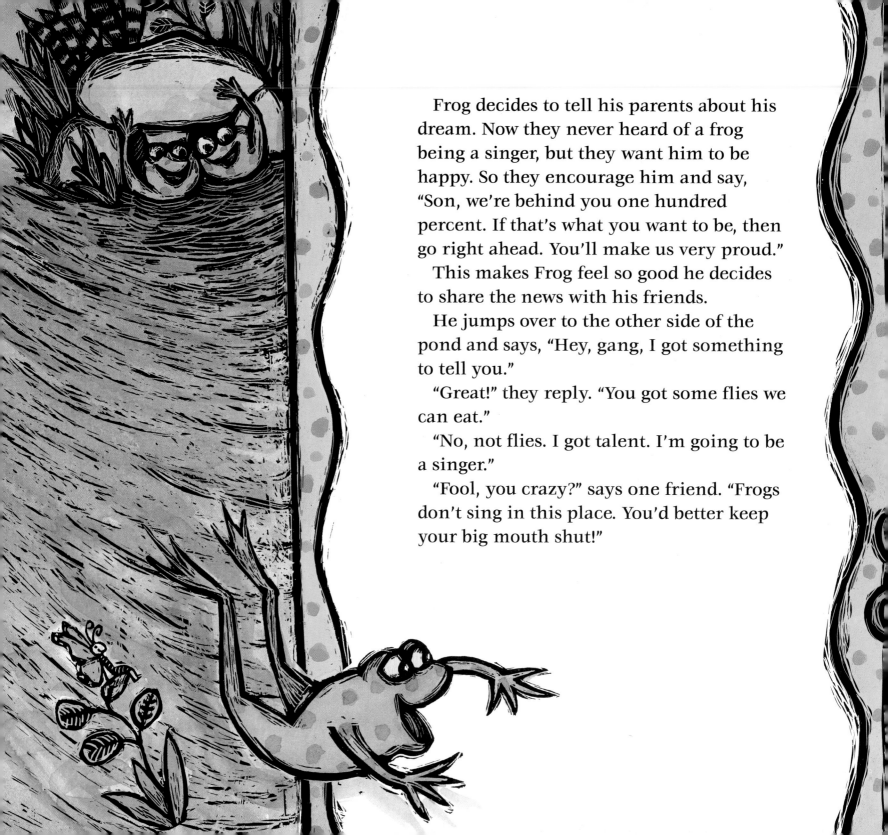

Frog decides to tell his parents about his dream. Now they never heard of a frog being a singer, but they want him to be happy. So they encourage him and say, "Son, we're behind you one hundred percent. If that's what you want to be, then go right ahead. You'll make us very proud."

This makes Frog feel so good he decides to share the news with his friends.

He jumps over to the other side of the pond and says, "Hey, gang, I got something to tell you."

"Great!" they reply. "You got some flies we can eat."

"No, not flies. I got talent. I'm going to be a singer."

"Fool, you crazy?" says one friend. "Frogs don't sing in this place. You'd better keep your big mouth shut!"

They laugh at Frog, so he jumps back over to his own lily pad.

Frog feels mighty bad, mighty sad, mighty mad, and mighty *frustrated*. He rocks back and forth and thinks about what to do. Finally he says to himself, "I know, I'll talk to the birds. Maybe they'll let me join their singing group."

He gathers up his confidence and hip hops over to the birds' house and knocks on their trunk. The head bird flies to the window and says, "Oh, it's the frog. How may we help you?"

Frog feels a little shy and begins to chew on his tongue. "Uh, well, you see," says Frog, "I would like to join your singing group."

"That's wonderful," says the head bird. "You may help us carry our worms."

"Worms?" says Frog. "That's not exactly what I had in mind. I—I—I—I—I want to—to—to sing wi-wi-with your group."

"Sing! An ugly-looking thing like you sing with us delicate creatures?" says the head bird. "Out! Out! Out you go!" And with that the birds flutter around Frog and throw him right out the door!

When Frog gets home, he wants to cry. He wants to give up. But he doesn't. Instead he just practices and practices and practices.

Then he begins to think, "The birds sing every night at the Big Time Weekly Concert, but it's Fox who's in charge."

And with one big leap, Frog jumps over to Fox's place.

"Brother Fox, it's me, Frog. I want to talk to you."

Now Fox really doesn't have time to be bothered by a frog.

"Quick, quick, quick, what do you want?" says the fox.

"I want to sing in the concert this Friday night," says Frog.

"A frog sing! Are you crazy? With that gravelly voice? Get out of here, quick, quick, quick."

"Please, Brother Fox, just give me a chance."

"Hmm," says Fox, shifting his eyes. "I can always use an opening act. Show up Friday night at eight o'clock sharp."

Monday rolls around,
Tuesday rolls around,
Wednesday rolls around,
Thursday rolls around—
and finally it is Friday.

Frog is so excited he
bathes all day. He scrubs
his little green fingers
and little green toes.

Oh, the frog is happy.
He is going to do his thing.
He is going to present
himself to the world.

He combs his hair, parts
it in the middle, and
slicks down the sides.

Then he looks down at his
reflection in the pond, smiles,
and says, "Um, um, um,
I am BEAUUUUTIFUL!
And tonight I am going to do
my thing!"

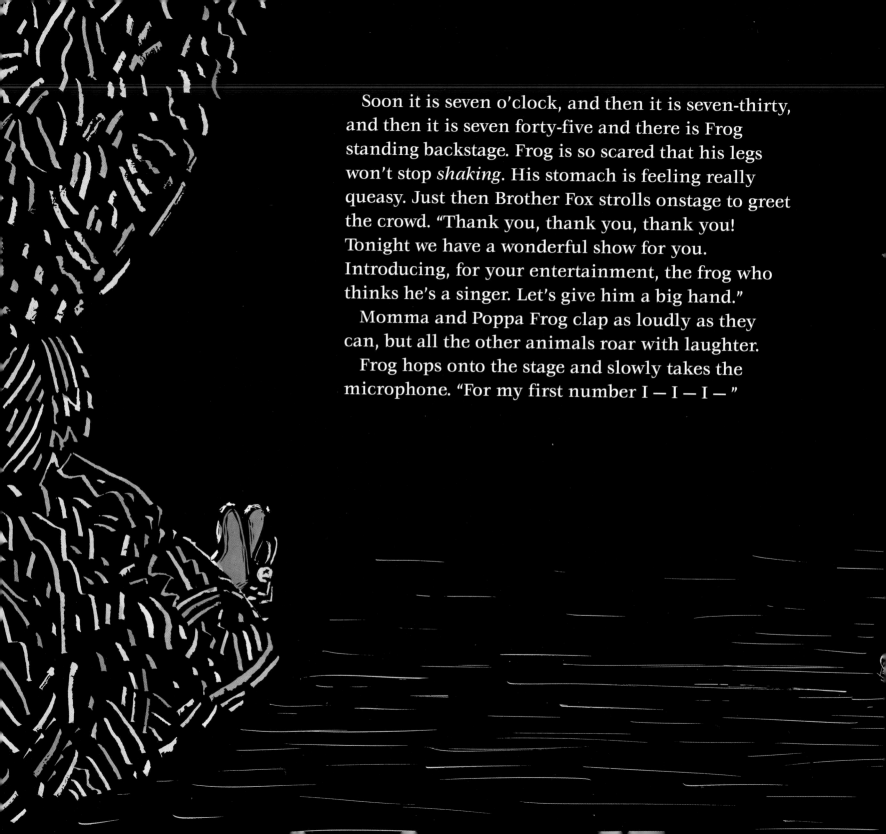

Soon it is seven o'clock, and then it is seven-thirty, and then it is seven forty-five and there is Frog standing backstage. Frog is so scared that his legs won't stop *shaking*. His stomach is feeling really queasy. Just then Brother Fox strolls onstage to greet the crowd. "Thank you, thank you, thank you! Tonight we have a wonderful show for you. Introducing, for your entertainment, the frog who thinks he's a singer. Let's give him a big hand."

Momma and Poppa Frog clap as loudly as they can, but all the other animals roar with laughter.

Frog hops onto the stage and slowly takes the microphone. "For my first number I — I — I — "

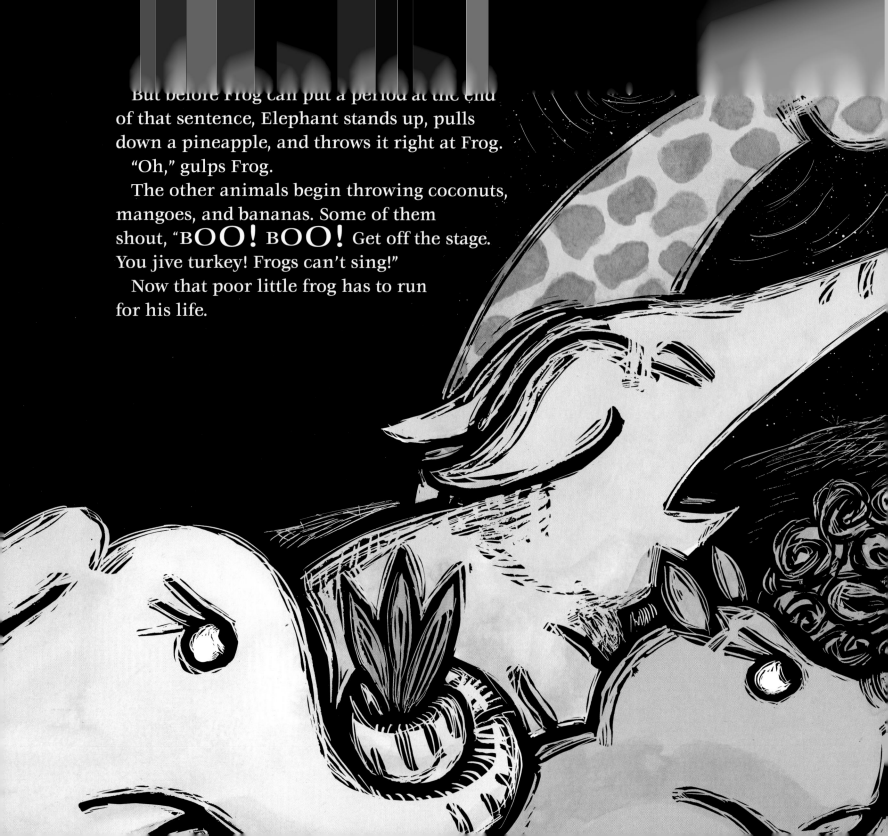

But before Frog can put a period at the end of that sentence, Elephant stands up, pulls down a pineapple, and throws it right at Frog.

"Oh," gulps Frog.

The other animals begin throwing coconuts, mangoes, and bananas. Some of them shout, "BOO! BOO! Get off the stage. You jive turkey! Frogs can't sing!"

Now that poor little frog has to run for his life.

Brother Fox rushes back onto the stage. "Okay, okay, okay, calm down—just trying out our comic routine. Now we have some *real* talent for your enjoyment. Presenting the birds, who can really sing."

The crowd claps as the birds fly onto the stage, their heads held high. They chirp, tweet, and whistle, causing the audience to fall into a soft, peaceful nod.

"This is more like it," whispers Elephant.

Everyone is resting quietly except Frog, who is tired of being pushed around.

He's tired of being FRUSTRATED.

He leaps over Brother Fox and hops back onto the stage. "I came here to sing my song tonight and that's just what I'm going to do!" he announces.

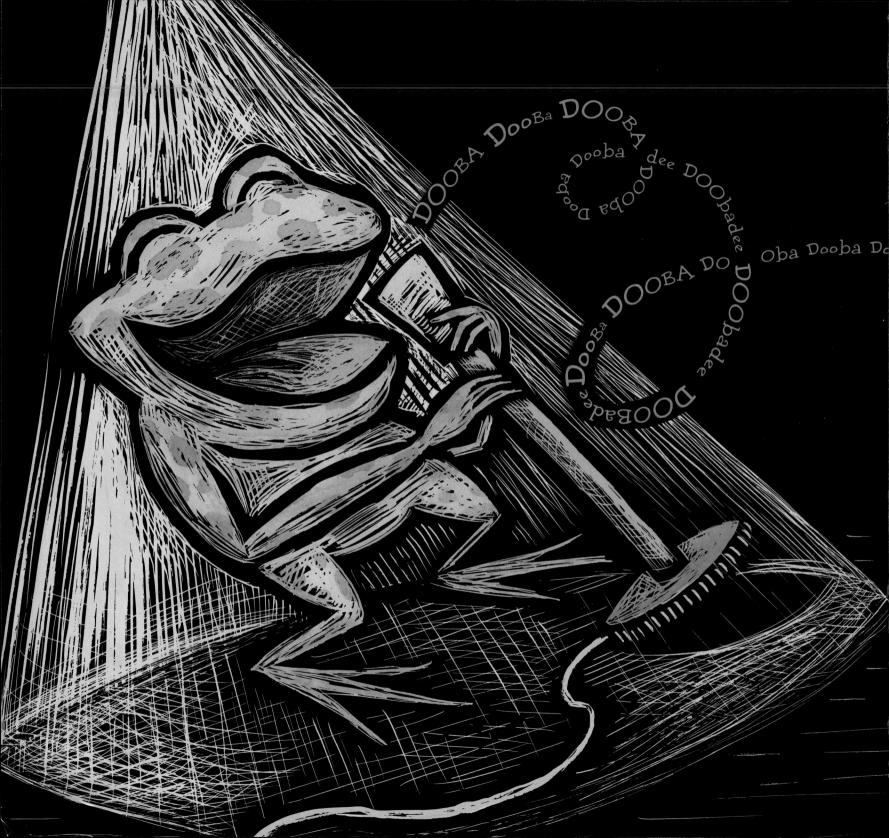

Frog takes a deep breath and, in the style of what we now call
Boogie-woogie, he bellows out:

"Dooba Dooba Dooba Dooba Dooba Dooba Dooba Dooba"

Frog bops his head about as though it were a jazzy saxophone.
His fingers move as though they were playing a funky bass fiddle.

"Dooba Dooba Dooba Dooba Doobadee Doobadee
Doobadee Doobadee"

Elephant opens one eye.
Then she opens the other eye.
And then she roars,
"Uuuuuuuuuuuuuuuuuumpht!
I do looooooooooove that
sound!" She swings her hips from
side to side and does a dance
we now call the bump.

Suddenly
Lion jumps up from
his seat. "I love it! I love
it!" he shouts. He shakes his
body thisaway and thataway
and every whichaway, doing a
dance we now call the twist.

Dooba Dooba Dooba ba Dooba Dooba
Doo dee DOObadee DOOba dee
Doobadee DOOBa DOOBA DOOba Dooba Doo
badee DOOBadee DOOBa Doo
DOOBadee Dooba DOOBa DOOBA Doobadee Dooba

Soon the snakes are boogalooing and the giraffes are doing the jerk. The hyenas do the slop and Fox does the mashed potato.

Even the birds want to join in: "We want to Dooba Dooba, too."

Tweet Tweet Tweet Dooba
Tweet Tweet Tweet Dooba

Now the whole forest is rocking. The joint is jumping. The animals are snapping their fingers and doing something they've never done before—they're dancing!

"Wow, Frog," shouts Brother Fox, "you are a genius. You have given us something new!"

From then on, Frog is allowed to sing every Friday night at the Big Time Weekly Concert. And, as my granddaddy used to say, *that* is how Rhythm and Blues was born.

Backstage Notes

The "dooba dooba" that Frog sings in the story is a Boogie-woogie tune. As the saying goes, the Boogie-woogie "ain't nothing but the Blues with dancing shoes on." A fast-paced, upbeat rhythm, it makes you want to snap your fingers and stomp your feet. Boogie-woogie is a form of Blues piano music popularized during the 1930s by the Boogie-woogie Trio: pianists Mead "Lux" Lewis, Albert Ammons, and Pete Johnson.

The Blues itself is rooted in Africa and is the foundation of American popular music. It was created by African Americans from the cotton fields, farm areas, cypress swamps, and backwoods of the South, especially along the Mississippi Delta. Musical forms and styles such as Country Blues, Classic Blues, City Blues, Urban Blues, Ragtime, Boogie-woogie, Harlem Stride, Jazz, Rhythm and Blues (R & B), Rock and Roll, Rap, and Pop music all grew out of the Blues. The Blues tells a story and expresses feelings of pain and joy. It allows one to improvise, to be spontaneous. The Blues awakens the creativity in our souls.

Acknowledgment

Special thanks to my editor, Melanie Kroupa, and designer, Chris Paul; my super agent, Carla Glasser; flutist Kathleen Kilpatrick, who transcribed the "dooba doobas" into music; my husband, Clay Goss, and his invaluable artistic advice; my assistant, Rhonda White; and illustrator Cynthia Jabar, who found a frog hiding in the Orchard.

Orchard Books
95 Madison Avenue
New York, NY 10016

Manufactured in the United States of America
Printed by Barton Press, Inc.
Bound by Horowitz/Rae
Book design by Chris Hammill Paul

10 9 8 7 6 5 4 3 2

The text of this book is set in 14 point Veljovic Medium.
The illustrations are scratchboard.

Library of Congress Cataloging-in-Publication Data

Goss, Linda.
The frog who wanted to be a singer / as told by Linda Goss ; illustrated by Cynthia Jabar.
p. cm.
"A Melanie Kroupa book" —
Half t.p.
Summary: The birds are the only animals that sing in the forest, but a frog with a powerful desire to make music gets his chance.
ISBN 0-531-06895-1. —
ISBN 0-531-08745-X (lib. bdg.)
[1. Frogs—Fiction. 2. Singers—Fiction. 3. Boogie woogie (Music)—Fiction.]
I. Jabar, Cynthia, ill. II. Title.
PZ7.G679Fr 1996
[E]—dc20

94-48803

A traditional Boogie-woogie pattern transcribed by Kathleen Kilpatrick.
The traditional Boogie-woogie pattern was originally played in the
bass clef by the left hand on the piano.